MY BLOODY VALENTINE

ROSE BUSH

My Bloody Valentine
Rose Bush

Copyright © 2021 Rose Bush All rights reserved

The characters and events portrayed in this book are fictitious. Any similarity to real persons, living or dead, is coincidental and not intended by the author.

No part of this book may be reproduced, or stored in a retrieval system, or transmitted in any form or by any means, electronic, mechanical, photocopying, recording, or otherwise, without express written permission of the publisher.

ISBN- 9798558872347

Cover design by: Rose Bush
Edited by: By Quill and Lantern Publishing

This book is dedicated to my husband Anthony. I love you.

HER CRUSH

COBEN

Today is the day. I am going to drop a letter into my crush's work mailbox. Hoping she feels the same as I do. Staying back in the shadows as an acquaintance has run its course.

I crave more.

I worked extremely hard on this letter and put hours of thought into it. I threw a little fake blood inside to show I know her favorite band—*My Bloody Valentine*. I even borrowed their lyrics, hoping she would get the pun.

Waverly's boss is my best friend from college. So far, he is the only person who knows of my minor obsession with her. Since he works with her all day, he gives me little pieces of information, like her favorite band. When she tattoos, she plays *My Bloody Valentine* on repeat. Who knew such a beautiful woman had such great taste in music.

Gorgeous is an understatement. Waverly's long black hair is sometimes messy yet looks beautiful no matter how she styles it. Her skin reminds me of peaches and cream. One day, I hope I'm lucky enough to taste her skin, to see if it's as delicious as it looks.

Her pouty lips perpetually wear a coat of black lipstick. I want to kiss and nibble them. She possesses expressive, almond-shaped hazel eyes—a knock out. I fell in love the first time I gazed into their depths.

I doubt she remembers our first encounter. Truthfully, I don't think she knows my real name. She uses my college nickname. Tripod.

♡

Three Years Ago

I walk into the shop expecting Ren to be at the front desk waiting for my appointment. Instead, I see this exquisite woman—long dark hair, black lipstick, soulful eyes, breathtaking beauty more blinding than the sun.

"Hi. Welcome to Tatted Canvas. Do you have an appointment today?"

Picking up my jaw off the floor and clearing my throat a few times, I'm finally able to speak. "Ummm, yes, I have an appointment with Ren today at eleven."

She clicked through the compute screens. "Ah-ha. Here you are. Tripod. Eleven with Ren for a cover-up."

"Uhhh," I stumble over my words. I want to correct the stupid nickname, but my brain and mouth refuse to coordinate.

"Ren!" she yells back. "Tripod is here."

"Come on back, man," Ren hollers.

"I'll walk you back. Is Tripod your real name?" She stares straight ahead, making small talk.

"I... No, no, it's not. It's a college nickname that seems to have stuck," I reply, praying she changes the conversation.

"Cool. Are you a photographer?"

"Yes. I am. I'd love to photograph you some time," I snapped my mouth closed as soon as I realized what I said. Way to sound like a fucking creep, I mentally kick myself. *"I mean if you are looking for a photographer."*

She giggles at my fumbling words.

"He is a photographer," Ren blurts with an evil smirk, *"but he earned the nickname another way—"*

"Stop!" I interrupt Ren. Please let him listen, for once in his life!

Ren ignores me. "His dick is so huge it looks like a tripod," Ren laughs his ass off.

"Dude, please stop," I beg, covering half my face with my palm.

"What? It is crucial information for the ladies." Ren shrugs as if he's serious.

"Where are my manners? Waverly, this is Tripod. And Tripod, this is the lovely Waverly, my new apprentice."

I shake her hand while hanging my head in embarrassment. But my head shoots up when I hear the most spellbinding sound. It's this captivating creature laughing. I have never listened to a more radiant sound.

Waverly throws up her hands. "I don't care to know how you know his dick size, Ren. Please don't go through the effort of trying to explain."

"All the ladies in college would rave about his sheer size," Ren continues to reminisce. *"Waverly, if you're interested in my man Tripod here, let me know. I'll hook ya up!"*

Trying to hold in her laughter, she manages, "I can get his information from the computer."

With a wink, she is gone.

ROSE BUSH

I SEE HER ONCE A MONTH, sometimes more often, since our initial meeting. I get work done or pop in to say hey to Ren. Other than that, we don't hang out. We have inconsequential conversations when she isn't swamped with customers.

She has a cat named Koopa the Troopa. However, Waverly only calls him Koopa. He is a tortoiseshell cat, and she loves Mario everything. She has an obsession with reading dark romance, and her favorite author is Pepper Winters.

During the last three years, she transformed from novice to a phenomenal and sought-after tattoo artist. I one day, I hope she'll tattoo me. The downside, I need to consciously downplay the hard-on I get any time she is near me. She always smells of vanilla and an exotic, unfamiliar bouquet of flowers.

Let's hope my love letter works its magic.

THE BLOODY VALENTINE

WAVERLY

Walking to the mailbox, I sniff the air basking in the crisp afternoon. February is a bipolar month in Ohio. It could be forty degrees, or it could be negative ten. It also could blizzard, or a soft rain, or vernal. Today I'm lucky to have spring-ish weather.

Grasping the mailbox's handle, I pull open the door and peer inside. No packages. I'm waiting for my new Bishop Rotary tattoo machine. I've never been good at waiting. Patience is not my virtue.

I grab the stack of letters and head inside to see what bills and bullshit the mail lady left. Most of the letters are junk, bills, or advertisements. Odd, one letter is in a thick envelope. My name is beautifully penned on the front: no return address or whatever.

It is rather strange this is in the tattoo shop's mailbox. Shrugging my shoulders, I grab the letter opener and slip it into the flap, slicing open the paper. Reaching my hand inside, I touch a damp piece of paper.

Looking down, I see a red substance on my hand. My heart begins to race. I know that substance too well.

Blood.

I feel faint. Not at the sight of blood, but the thought of someone else's blood sent to me in the mail. I think of a dozen reasons why blood could on the letter and settle on a bloody nose. *Why wouldn't they stop or rewrite the letter?* I shake my head at the absurd thoughts. *A bloody nose, seriously?*

This calms me somewhat, so I don't call the police but read the letter. Unfolding the stained letter, my heart drops when I read the words:

Waverly,

> I have a lot to say. I've held everything in for far too long. You have licked me with your fire. My heart is burning up. You control these feelings. My love for you grows daily, like a raging inferno. I watch you from a distance, praying you will one day notice me. You will be mine by Valentine's day. Loving you from a distance is no longer an option.
>
> Your Valentine Crush.

Stalker. The stalker used lyrics from my favorite songs. Not everyone knows the lyrics to My Bloody Valentine's music. They may recognize the name of the band, but that's about it. They are an 80's band. If the band isn't talking about twerking, sex, or food—my generation doesn't listen to it.

"Anything good in the mailbox?" Ren asks, scaring me out of my musings.

"Mostly bills and ads," I say in a distracted voice.

"What's that in your hand? Is that blood?" he asks, alarmed.

I give him the letter. "Yea, it is. Read this and tell me what you think."

He is quiet while reviewing the paper. His face is scrunched up in concentration. "I think this guy or girl is a creep."

"Do you think I should call the police and make a report?"

"Have you felt like anyone was watching you? Had any bad dates, obsessive boyfriends, or anyone giving you unwanted attention?"

"No, none of that. I don't date often." Scratching my head, I can't think of any perverts. "My last partner and I split, but it was mutual."

Ren sighs, "Put it in a zip-lock bag for now, and if you continue to get creepy-ass gifts, then we will make a report. Also, write the date down that you received it in case you have to make a report. You know the police around here, they won't act unless they're standing in the pile of shit."

Nodding, I head to wash my hands before grabbing a plastic bag. The blood is slick, not sticky. I sniff my fingers and realize it's fake. Too chemical, and it lacks the familiar coppery scent.

"I'll walk you to your car every night, even if I've to make a client wait. Your safety is important."

"Thank you, but I don't think that is necessary. It is fake blood. Give it a whiff."

Curious, Ren put his nose to the paper and inhales. "Damn,

what a freak. Still, no arguments, don't go alone outside," he states and walks away before I can protest. I don't need a damn babysitter. I'm 25-years-old.

I return to the front desk to check the appointments. Like clockwork, I see it's Tripod's monthly appointment: eleven on the dot. A man after my own heart, I love schedules and not being late. I'm a creature of habit.

Just thinking of seeing him makes me hot. His hair alone, the messy throwback quiff, long on top and a high skin fade on the sides, makes my fingers itch. He has a silver hoop in his nose. I've never thought a nose piercing on a man would actually be sexy, but it works on him.

Tattoos all over his gorgeously fit body. At least I *assume* they cover his body. From what I have seen in person, my imagination fills in the gaps hidden by his clothing.

It makes me drool thinking of his nickname. *Tripod, not because he is a photographer but because his dick is huge.* Ren's words, not mine. I have seen him come in with his gray sweatpants on. They left nothing to the imagination.

Tripod's eyes are coppery in color with flecks of green, gold, and brown. They look into your soul and make you feel like he sees all of your deepest and darkest secrets. They make me feel accepted, safe, and—loved? I'm not sure about the love part; that is a strong word, maybe a *strong liking*.

The bell jingles above the door, warning someone entered the lobby. I look up to a smiling Tripod.

"Hey," he gives his signature smooth greeting.

"Hey, Tripod. You can go on back. Ren is waiting on you," I gesture towards the back.

"You're looking flushed. Are you okay? Got a fever?"

Placing my hands on my cheeks, trying to hide my blush, I say, "I'm just a little warm, that's all."

"You should go outside. It feels great out there. I was able to finally wear basketball shorts today." He gestures towards his shorts.

My face flushes hotter. Through the material of Tripod's jogging shorts, the outline of his cock hangs down his left leg. I see the soft ridges and veins, no way he wears boxers or briefs. To hide the fact gawked at his penis, I focus on the computer. Clearing my throat, I say, "I will do that. You better head back. I don't want to make you late."

"Chat later."

"You bet." I rush back to the restroom when he is out of sight.

I wash the fake blood off my hands with soap and water. Then splash water on my face to cool off my raging hormones. That man is a walking fantasy.

DOZENS OF ROSES

COBEN

I noticed the dried blood on her hands when I walked in. She got my Valentine's day letter. She was flushed, the same way I imagine she looks when she reaches orgasm. And yes, I have imagined it plenty of times.

The way she examined my shorts gave me a semi. Trying to conceal it from Ren is rough. Knowing Waverly wants me, well, I want to double my efforts to make her mine.

"Dude. Put that heat-seeking moisture missile away. Waverly won't date you if you scare her away with that huge thing pointing at her like she is under attack," Ren chuckles.

"Shut the fuck up," I grumble at him.

"Don't get all pissy on me. Are you on your monthly?" he jokes.

I flip him the bird. "Fuck off."

Shaking his head, Ren takes it in stride. "What are you getting done today, soldier?"

"You're the artist, do what you want. I want it right here," I say, pointing to an empty spot on my chest.

"Whatcha getting?" Waverly peers in the room and asks.

"I don't know. I figured I would give Ren some creative freedom."

"Can I draw it? I have the perfect idea." She leans against the door frame, leaning forward to view my chest.

"Sure," I shrugged, acting nonchalant. Watching her staring gives me goosebumps. The way her eyes trail up and down my body, it feels like she's caressing me.

"You're going to trust me? Just like that?" She asks, walking towards me.

I reply, "You were trained by the best. Ren wouldn't let you fuck up."

"Can I connect it to your skull?" She touches the skin beneath where I want the new tattoo. It's an older tat, a life-like rendering of a skull.

"Yeah, why not?" I say, managing to hide a shiver.

She grabs the phone from her pocket and takes a photo. "I'll be back. I have to go sketch it out." She rushes out of the room.

To control my heartbeat and my dick, I inhale steadying breaths. But my damn dick isn't listening. Waverly's scent lingers in the room. I wish I could bottle up her scent and carry it with me. It is intoxicatingly sexy.

Twenty minutes later, she returns, out of breath from running and excitement. *Is that what she sounds like when she makes love?* Those thoughts cause my dick to flutter. *Down boy!*

Waverly lifts her sketch. She incorporates the skull, adds bright red blood spatter and abstract lines in the background, layers of colorful arabesque flowers, and deepens the skull's black definition. Worry creases her brows, and she bites her bottom lip with her top teeth.

"It's fucking awesome," I proclaim, accepting the sketch. I'm not big on flowers, but these aren't feminine. They look deadly, poisonous. "Thank you, Waverly."

"You're welcome," she beams. "I'll get out of your hair so Ren can get to tattooing you."

"What do you mean, *Ren*? You're the one who designed it. You have to tattoo it."

"I can't; You're Ren's client. I have a client coming in—" she checks her watch, "ten minutes."

"Then make an appointment with you, and I will get it done then," I reply. "I've plenty of spots open for Ren to work on."

She shakes her head. "No. I refuse to take Ren's clients."

"Waverly, I don't care. Make his appointment. I will do a different tattoo today," Ren interjects before she can argue.

"Fine. I have an opening on Valentine's day, but it's at 3:00 pm. Does that work for you?" She checks her phone. "If not, my next opening isn't for three weeks."

"Valentine's day works for me."

Eyeing me, she states, "No plans with your partner? Valentine's day is two days away if you count today. Wouldn't want you in the dog house over a sweet ass tattoo."

"My plans are a new sweet ass tattoo. I don't have a girlfriend or a wife." I smile at her.

"Sounds good. Gotta go get everything ready for my client. Have a good session, Tripod."

"It's Coben."

"What?" she asks at the door.

"My name is Coben. You don't have to keep calling me Tripod."

"Nice name. But I'll just keep calling you Tripod. It seems to be fitting." Her eyes drift down to my shorts.

I laugh and choke at the same time. I had never heard her make an inappropriate joke. Or was that a sexual innuendo? Ren shakes his head and trying to contain his laughter.

"What?" I ask.

"You two." He nods his head toward the open door. "I don't know why you two don't hook up already."

As I pull on my shirt, I manage, "Waverly is more than a hookup."

"Or date. Whatever. The sexual tension is so fucking thick. I'm ready to die of suffocation."

"Drama queen."

"Pussy," he jabs back.

"I am what I eat." I shrug.

Putting on a pair of gloves, Ren chuckles, "That was a terrible joke."

"If it was so terrible, then why are you laughing."

"Man, it was fucking terrible, but funny. Now, where are we tattooing?"

I point to a spot on my leg needing covered. Slowly, I've replaced horrible drunken tattoos with Ren's work. He should cover them. To be fair, he did most of them while he was an apprentice.

While I hear the buzz of the tattoo gun and feel the first zap of the needle, I get my phone. Lying on my stomach, it's time to start phase two of wooing Waverly. I order one dozen black roses, one dozen red roses, and one dozen orange roses for delivery tomorrow afternoon. Black roses are to represent a significant change. The red roses represent true love, romance, and desire; kind of unoriginal, but I'm trying. And the orange roses are to express desire and fascination. Orange is also her favorite color, which is a plus.

I chose random black vases for the flowers. Wrote another anonymous note, but I hope it gives Waverly a hint her admirer is me. Relaxing into the tattoo chair, I imagine her surprise and excitement. All this love and attention I'm paying her—I mean, *her crush* is paying her, what girl wouldn't swoon?

SPECIAL DELIVERY

WAVERLY

When I go to check the mailbox, my heart races, I'm not sure if it's from fear or excitement. After thinking long and hard about the bloody valentine, I'm not sure how to feel. I'm flattered but also scared the person could be a stalker. Knowing that much about me—well, it's freaky.

Instant relief hits when no anonymous letters wait to ambush me. Maybe that means no stalker, just a crush.

Back inside, I give the mail to Ren.

"Any creeper letters?" he asks, sorting through advertisements.

"Nope. I'm hoping it means it's a one and done. Could have been a joke from a friend."

"Sure," he half-heartedly agrees.

We get work stocking supplies and prepping for our clients. When the bell above the door jingles. I walk out and give my customary greeting. "Welcome to Tatted Canvas. Do you have an appointment today?"

"No, ma'am, just a delivery. Is there a Waverly here?"

"*Ahhh*, yeah. I'm Waverly," I say in excitement. *Finally! My new tattoo gun.*

"Alright," he says while checking his order sheet, "let me grab your stuff."

He and his partner walk in with three bouquets of roses stuffed into black vases: black, red, and the last is orange.

The vases resemble urns stuffed with black roses.

The whole thing freaks me the fuck out. Black roses represent death and mourning. I can't think of any other reason to send them except for a funeral or a death in the family. Even then, I would choose lilies.

The red and orange roses are beautiful. Red roses are romantic and slightly tacky. They are the go-to flower men pick out when they have no idea what flowers their date likes. To me, the orange blooms are the most unique and prettiest. Whoever sent these must have known it was my favorite color.

Bending down to sniff the petals, I search for a note. It is connected to the black roses. I slide it from the envelope, glad to see no blood. Unfolding it slowly, my heart hammering in my chest.

Waverly,

> Black roses can represent death.
> That may be true as you stole my breath.
> The blood on your hand.
> I hope you didn't misunderstand.

My love for you is true.
Take this as another clue.

Your Valentine Crush.

I have to admit my *Valentine Crush* has a lot of game. He or she put in the leg work, figuring out what I like, writing me a poem. I've wracked my brain, trying my damnedest to figure out the person's identity. I don't have a ton of friends. I have clients, but none of them have openly hit on me or displayed any kind of romantic interest.

My best friend Laken says people hit on me *all the time*. I'm not an idiot. I can tell the difference between innocent flirting, a common occurrence at the shop, and the real thing. I guess I'm used to it.

As I work, my mind settles on the stalker—I mean *Valentine Crush*. I blast through most of my clients with casual small talk, half-paying attention to their replies. My last appointment is with Laken. Looking at my phone, I see I got a text from her a few minutes ago.

Laken- Hey girl. I'm going to be late.
Me- How late? You're my last of the day. I'm not trying to stay here all night.
Laken- Just 5 minutes. My alarm didn't go off.
Me- OK, L. See you soon.

Waiting for Laken to arrive, I munch on a light snack. Shoving the last five Black Forest gummy worms into my mouth, I peek in the empty bag wishing for more.

"You didn't save me any?"

"Hell no. I don't share my worms with anyone." I glare at Ren.

He holds his heart, feigning hurt. "Jerk. I feel the love."

The bell sounds above the door. "You want to go grab my next client?" I ask Ren.

"Sure," he replies, surprising me. "Be right back."

Their voices are slightly muffled, but I can hear everything.

"Hey Laken, long time no see."

"Hey... Ren. Yea... long time. How have you been?"

"Oh, you mean these last two weeks, after you ghosted me?"

"Ren," she hesitates.

"Don't worry about it. I am fine. Waverly is waiting for you."

"Will you let me explain?"

"No need. You ghosting someone pretty much gets your point across," he says in a voice filled with hurt.

Silence follows his heart-wrenching words. Nothing. Then I hear Laken's heels clicking on the floor coming towards my doors. I grab the last of my supplies, acting as if I wasn't eavesdropping on their conversation.

"You bitch. That was a dirty trick you just pulled," Laken accuses, walking into my room and closing the door.

Wiping down the chair with mint-smelling cleaner, I look at her. "What? I asked him to get my next client. I do it for him all the time."

"You know we went on a date a few weeks ago." Her hand is on her hip. "I told you what happened."

"I do know some of what went down," I agree and toss the paper towel into the trash. "I think you're scared to get close to Ren. He mopes when nobody is around. I see how much you hurt him. You're my best friend, but you did him dirty."

"I didn't mean to hurt him. It's just... with my history; I couldn't drag him through my drama-filled life. Even if he is the dreamiest man, I've ever tasted."

"Tasted!" I screech and then cover my mouth. "You and Ren did the dirty? I want to ask questions, but I don't want those pictures in my head. Thinking of my boss naked, no—bad idea."

"You should. He is fucking hot. The carpet matches the drapes." She wiggles her eyebrows. "Ten glorious…"

"Stop! I don't want the details. Please stop," I stick my fingers in my ears to block out her next words. I see her mouth say *inches*. "*Lalala*, I can't hear you."

"Very mature, Waverly," she says with an eye roll and laughs.

"Never said I was mature," I assert. "I do, however, want the reason why the fuck you ghosted Ren. He has been pining over you since you first met. And you've done the same."

She frowns. "Preston."

"Are you fucking kidding me? Why would you let Preston back into your life? He cheated on you."

"I can't help who I love, Waverly." She acts like Preston is the fucking sun, and she's trapped in his gravitational pull.

"We have this fight every time we talk about him," I say, and I'm not wrong. "I'll drop it. But you need to stop hurting people over Preston."

"You're right, and thanks." She plops her purse in the corner. "What has been going on with you? We haven't spoken in a few days, and I'm sorry about that."

"That's okay. I've been pretty busy with clients and stalkers."

"Stalkers?" she asks in an alarmed voice.

"It's nothing serious. Just a bloody valentine and three dozens of roses in urns with a poem."

"Bloody valentine?" Her mouth hangs open. "Like real blood?"

Laying down plastic on my work table, I shake my head. "Fake blood, at least I think it was anyway. It didn't have the coppery scent like real blood, and it stained my hands. Get on the chair so we can get started," I instruct.

"Fuck. Seeing blood anywhere gives me the heebie-jeebies." She shivers in disgust.

Tapping the gun, I listen to the buzzing purr. "Yet here you are getting a tattoo. That will bleed *blood*," I chuckle.

"That is different," she huffs.

"No, not really."

Ignoring me, she continues. "Anyways, what did the letters say? The roses are beautiful, even the black ones." She looks at them sitting over on my counter.

I retrieve the zip-loc bags with the two letters and let her read them as I continue the delicate line work on her hip tattoo. We have been working on this tattoo for months. The hip to breast tattoo starts at her pelvis, winds its way around her leg, and travels to her breast. The cherry's branches and delicate blossom are a physical manifestation of moving on from her past. This is a unique way of showing how this frail and fragile woman transformed herself.

"Wow, Waverly, this guy sounds fucking creepy. *You will be mine by valentine's day*. What a psycho. What're you going to do about him?"

"Nothing," I reply. "He is probably a guy with a crush. He has only sent these gifts. Nothing more. Not like he's following me around town, peeping in my windows."

"Are you sure?"

Damn. I assumed he wasn't peeping in my windows. "Yes?"

"Waverly," she scolds. "You can't assume he isn't following you. You should probably call the cops."

"I will if anything else happens. Ren walks me to my car every night."

"Promise?"

"Promise!"

We stick to small talk for the rest of her appointment. After setting my gun down, I sit back and admire this shiny new ink.

Using a damp cloth, I wipe away the blood rising to the skin. "It's finally finished."

"Seriously?" Laken twists, trying to see. "I never expected it to be done. Months of visits, it felt never-ending."

"Seriously. It is so beautiful. Go look in the mirror." I motion at my floor to ceiling mirror.

The door opens. "Hey, Waverly. How much longer will you—" Ren's words are cut off as he looks at Laken. "Sorry. But damn Laken, that looks awesome as fuck."

"Thank you," she blushes, not caring if Ren sees her almost naked body.

"Another twenty minutes. I need to get her tattoo cleaned and wrapped up. Then I have to clean up my room. If you need to leave, go ahead," I say, tossing my used gloves away and heading to the sink to wash my hands.

Laken says, "I can walk her to her car."

"I can wait. It wouldn't be very gentlemanly to let two classy women walk to their cars alone." He gives a side smile.

When did I become a child again? "Thanks, but I don't need a babysitter."

"You don't get a choice, Waverly. We talked about this. Your safety is important." He turns to leave the room, but not before I see him adjusting his pants.

"Bossy fucker," I huff.

"It is hot as fuck too," Laken states, fanning herself.

Grumbling in irritation, I don a new pair of gloves to finishing up with Laken. Then, I deep clean my room. Ren walks us to our cars. We wave goodbye and head our separate ways.

THE PACKAGE

COBEN

Ren and I meet for drinks after work.

"Hey man, how was slinging ink?" I ask Ren. He looks tired as hell.

"It was rough. I had a client trying to tell me how to do my job. As if I haven't been tattooing for years, and let's not mention I'm the owner of the damn shop," he rants. "Waverly received flowers and a poem. Then she asks me later if I will go grab her last client of the day. Low and behold, it is fucking Laken. We got into a sort of argument, and she was trying to explain why she had fucking ghosted me."

"Damn, man. That sounds rough. Let's order greasy ass food with beers," I suggest.

"Best suggestion I've heard all day."

Laken and Ren went out on a date around a month ago. Poor guy, he believed she was *the one*. Then she went and ghosted him: no explanation or anything.

Poof. Gone.

I've never seen a woman get to Ren like Laken. It has to seriously suck that she is Waverly's friend. Seeing her in the shop all the time must be hell. Ren is a real gentleman, though; he'd not refuse Waverly a client.

At a table, we order our food and a pitcher of beer to share. We sit in companionable silence until our beers arrive. The server sets it down and says our meal will be out soon. I pour us both a glass, and we take hearty sips.

"You wanna talk about the Laken thing?" I ask.

"Not really, but I know if I don't, I will hold it in until I break." He holds his mug of beer between his hands.

"I'm here." I stare at the bubbles in the amber fluid. "Tell me what she said today."

"Not much. I wouldn't let Laken give me some bullshit excuses as to why she would ghost someone. I told her the action pretty much gets the point across."

"I agree." And I do agree; I'm not Laken's biggest fan. "I don't understand why she couldn't just tell you it was over or whatever."

"She should have. I texted her daily for a week after our date. She never answered them. So, like every other normal person, I got the hint. We fucked, and then she left me." Frustrated, he sips his beer. "I did hear her and Waverly speaking about Preston."

The name sounded familiar. "Her ex? I thought she left the cheating douche bag."

He threw up his hands. "That is what I thought too. After I heard that I had to leave my room, those thin walls can be a blessing or a curse."

"I'm sorry, man. I truly am." I wait, allowing for an appropriate pause between conversations. "You mentioned Waverly got some flowers?"

"Dude, yeah, she has a weirdo crush sending her gifts." He rubs his jaw, thinking. "It's honestly not my business, but you know, I keep an eye on her. Enough of my bullshit. How was your day?"

"Slow. Model shoot for a magazine and I did a few family pictures." My job isn't exciting. Honestly, it can be a real pain in the ass. Directing selfish models to look one way, stand another, show more cleavage, and the whole racket isn't my passion but pays the bills.

Ren lifts his near-empty glass to me. "I'm proud of the amazing photographer you have become. Fuck, I knew you wouldn't give up doing family portraits when you hit the big leagues."

"Why stop what got me to where I am? I love offering good quality pictures to families for a great price." We clink glasses. "Keeps me humble."

Our food arrives, and we eat in silence. We watch the football game on the TV above the bar, occasionally commenting on the players. After finishing our food, beer, and football, we say our goodbyes and make plans to hang out again.

I drive home with a smile. Waverly got my flowers. I'm assuming she loved them. If Laken's presence hadn't shaken up Ren, I would have gotten more information on the delivery.

With that thought, I stop at the store instead of going straight home. I get a large shopping basket and start browsing the Valentine's Day aisles. Looking at the cheesy items, my stomach churns. Of course, men would get their women red appliances with hearts all over them.

What woman, in reality, wants appliances? They want and *need* romance. I go through every aisle in the store. Two hours later, my basket is full, and I'm ready to check out. I put everything into my truck and go home.

In my kitchen, I endeavor to put everything I bought Waverly into a box. Thankfully I hang out at the shop so much. I know her favorite snacks, color, things she likes, and I know her favorite books. I ordered two gifts online.

Carefully wrapping them, I package everything up, and I place them into the box. I sit to write another letter. I seal it in the box.

I write her name on the outside and send a silent prayer that she accepts me when she finds out I'm her crush.

The next morning I have to be up early to do photoshoots with a company. I leave with time to spare to drop the large box off at Tatted Canvas.

LARGE PARCEL

WAVERLY

I'M RUNNING A FEW MINUTES LATE THIS MORNING. IT'S MY OWN damn fault. I needed an extra boost that only espresso provides. So I skipped my coffee pot and drove out of my way for a triple shot of espresso over ice.

Worth it.

After parking my car, I sit for a moment and sip my jet fuel. Deciding I better get my ass inside to prepare for today's clients, I begrudgingly get out of the car and head to the front door to unlock the shop. I notice a large box with my name on it.

I give it a light nudge with my shoe, preparing to run if anything ticks. *Like I could run from a damn bomb.* Shaking my head at my ridiculous thoughts, I go inside and set all my stuff down. Then I return to the front door and grab the box. Bringing it inside, I sit it on the front coffee table by the couch in the lobby.

Cautiously opening the box, I peer inside. It is a box full of random goodies. The first thing that catches my eye is the two big one-pound bags of my favorite Black Forest gummy bears. I squeal in excitement.

Digging even further is a black pillow with red lettering. The pillow reads *Fuck Valentine's Day, I love you every day*. The red lettering resembles blood drops. Cool but creepy. A bouquet of slim jims, another favorite snack, has me doing a shimmy.

At the bottom, there are two wrapped gifts and a card. I remove them from the box and set the box on the floor. First, I pick up the card, my name scrolled in the same handwriting on the front.

The front of the card reads: *Stalker is a harsh word*.
I hold my breath. The inside reads: *I prefer Valentine*.

Waverly,

Fuck Valentine's Day. I will love you every day. I got you the pillow as a daily reminder, so you will never forget my love for you is true. Cuddle with the printed message and think of me. Snack on your favorite snacks and know that I pay attention to everything you do. Enjoy the ink and words, think of me when you tattoo, and relax. Tomorrow is the day I will make you mine. Be ready for my last gift. Myself.

Love.
Your Valentine Crush.

Ink? Words? What the hell is this creep talking about? The last gift is himself? What the hell?

I tear away the black cobweb wrapping paper. The design is cool, better than the regular Valentine's Day hearts. It fits better with my favorite holiday, Halloween. I suspect my Valentine Crush figured that out too.

The package is tall and solid. Taking a deep breath, I pull the gift wrap back, and I squeal in utter delight when I see it is my favorite series by Pepper Winters in paperback. And they are signed! I hug the books to my chest.

"What the hell is all of this?"

"Ah! Holy shit, Ren. You scared me!" I say with a scream.

"Sorry I was running late. Why are you all giddy, like a schoolgirl? " he asks with a lift of a red eyebrow.

"My stalker has hit again," I hold up my books, "but with gifts."

"I am guessing they are good gifts." He leans forward. "You sound excited, not creeped out."

"So fucking good. I still have one more thing to open. But I'm not sure how it could get any better."

Tearing open the last package, all I can do is yell, "*Holy fucking shit.*"

"Is that ink?" Ren asks.

My hand roams over the bottles. "The exact brand that I use. I don't have all of these colors. This set alone is almost two hundred bucks."

"Damn. Your stalker knows you, no question. If he knows your brand, that means he's been here and in your room."

The idea makes me shiver. *Well, there goes my happy bubble.* "That doesn't mean anything. I always have Slim Jims, gummy bears, and my ink sitting out on my desk. Anyone who comes here would know those things," I rationalize. "He also wrote this letter."

He reads it, and his eyes grow wide. "You're going to have to cancel your appointments tomorrow. I can't have you here, and he gets to you."

"I have one appointment tomorrow with Tripod."

"He is your only appointment? You said you had that one appointment open for the next three weeks?"

"Tomorrow is my day off." I show him the schedule. "I planned on coming in for him."

Ren frowns.

"What? He is your friend. I was accommodating," I defended.

"Alright," he concedes, " since Tripod will be here. We can both protect you from the stalker if needed."

"Thank you, *Dad*," I reply in exasperation.

"Waverly. Don't be a child. I'm just looking out for you."

"I know." Sighing, I put my arm around his bicep. "Look, I'm just not used to it. The stalker thing, I still think it's a joke, you know."

He pats me on the head like a dog. "You better get used to it. Tripod and I won't let anything bad happen. Joke or not, if it doesn't stop, we go right to the police tomorrow. Maybe nothing happens, and it's all a gag, but shit, you never know."

"I appreciate the concern, I do. Enough about stalkers and sappy talk. Let's get to fucking work," I say, putting my stuff in the box and carrying it to my room.

Around lunchtime, I hear a familiar voice in the front area. I finish cleaning my equipment and station before going out to say hello.

"*Tri-pod*," I say in a sing-song voice.

"Hey, Waverly. How are you?" he asks while bending down and hugging me.

"Pretty good. Are you ready for your tattoo tomorrow?"

"You won't hurt me, will you?" he teases. Then, he lifts a bag up. "I hope you're hungry. I brought tacos."

"Starving. Thanks for bringing lunch." I peer inside the take-out bag. "Were you in the area?"

Tripod leaned on the counter. "I took the rest of the day off. I need to work on a special project."

"Nice. How much do I owe you for lunch?"

"Don't worry about it. You will just have to buy me lunch," he winks.

Swoon. This sexy man is so fucking thoughtful. I wish he was my crush. I highly doubt it. He isn't the secretive and stalker type. He is brilliant, talented, outspoken, and perfect. He would be the ideal book boyfriend, but I'm sure he has flaws I just don't see or choose not to see them.

We eat lunch and chat about his latest assignments. He did a catalog shoot for an underwear company. He described it as a walking fantasy—and that right there is why Tripod isn't the perfect book boyfriend. He probably only has one night stands. I can't turn a hoe into a house husband. Not that I want a house husband, or do I?

I bring out a bag of my gummy worms and share it. I may have said I don't share with anyone, but he bought me tacos. How could I not share my snacks with him? Ren again acts hurt, so I share with him too.

Thirty minutes later, I'm washing my hands and getting ready for my next appointment. Tripod heads out to his *special project* or whatever he has to go do, and Ren takes a power nap.

The rest of the day is average. I keep thinking about my new gifts. I've been itching to get my ass home and read my books. I have already read them, but I haven't read the paperbacks yet. And yes, there is a difference between reading an eBook and a paperback.

At the end of the night, Ren walks me to my car, and I go home, shower, and dive into my books.

SPECIAL PROJECT

COBEN

The special project came from the look of pure unadulterated lust on Waverly's face. When she looked at my cock outline in my basketball shorts, a lightbulb moment went off in my head the next day. I'm hoping this isn't going too far. I was initially going for a *Clone-A-Willy,* but I saw an advertisement for a *Cockolate.* It is a *Clone-A-Willy* Valentine's limited edition chocolate cock.

I felt like it was meant to be. It's sexy but funny.

I may have purchased a second one for Ren. If he wishes, he can make one for Laken. I know they will eventually get together, and he will need it. Plus, limited edition means it's going to be a collector's item. Right?

I pull everything out of the box and start to read the directions. Making sure to do this right and not to fuck it up.

1. Be prepared: Get everything set up before you start the process. Make sure to have a penis pump or penis

ring to help you stay harder for longer if needed. Ask someone special to help you to make it fun and sexy. Warning! If you are larger than average, you may need more silicon and chocolate to fill the mold.
2. Cut the tube to size. Do this by placing your erect penis next to the tube and marking the side with a marker. Warning! Do NOT cut while your penis is in or near the tube. If you have a curved penis see instructions section 2B for cutting instructions.
3. Mix 1 ¾ cup of warm water (98 degrees F) with the packet of silicon. Mix for 60 seconds.
4. Place the erect penis into the cut tube. Slowly pour the silicone mixture into the tube. Let sit for 2 minutes. Carefully remove the penis. After the mold has hardened for 20 minutes. Cut the tube off of the mold.
5. Melt all chocolate and fill your mold. Place in the fridge for 6 hours before removing it from the mold. Enjoy your nice hard Cockolate.

SEEMS EASY ENOUGH. I set all of my stuff in order. I don't have a pump or ring, but thoughts of Waverly keep me hard all damn day. Just thinking her name has me hard as a rock. I remove my pants and get the tube measured out, and start cutting, away from my penis, of course.

Mixing the silicone and water without wearing pants makes me think I should have done this in my bathroom. This is going to be messy. I would hate to mess up the rug in my kitchen. I'm glad I remembered to close the blinds. I only imagine the show the neighbors might get if I'd have forgotten.

I mix the silicone and then place my dick, which is still hard, into the tube. I pour the silicon and set a timer. I hear the click of the lock on the front door. I try not to panic, but I'm standing in my kitchen with my dick out. I need to keep thinking of Waverly. *Don't go soft.*

There are only two people with a key. I pray it isn't my mother. Thinking of my mother causes me to deflate. *Don't go soft!*

"Hey, Tripod! What's up, man?" Ren asks but stops when he sees me in the kitchen.

"Hey..."

I went soft.

Damn open concept floor plan. Why did I think it was a good idea when I bought the house?

"What the fuck are you doing? Are you jacking off in your kitchen?" Ren drops his shoulder bag by the door and closes it. "Dude, please tell me you aren't. We sit at that kitchen island and eat."

"No, I'm working on a special project."

"Jacking off isn't a special project, dude. I know you just had lunch with Waverly and me but damn, dude."

Frustrated, I lean my head back and stare at the ceiling. "I'm not jacking off. I was making a clone of my dick, if you must know."

"Gross. Are you into some kinky shit? You know what, don't answer that. I don't want to fucking know. I just came over to order dinner since you brought us lunch earlier. Now I am rethinking my choice."

"It's nothing kinky." I pause. *Isn't it, though?* "It's a Valentine's Day gift. I got you one too." I lift the unopened package.

"Valentine's day gift for who? And one for me? Who the fuck would I make a clone of my dick for?" He squints at the package and starts laughing. "Does that say *Cockolate*?"

"It's my grand finale. And yes, I got you one to make one for Laken. You two will be together eventually."

"Grand finale for?" He urges me to tell him, motioning with

his arms. "Laken and I will never be a thing. I learned my lesson."

"For Waverly," I say in a rush. "And we will see. I would say let's bet on it, but I will let you keep your money."

"It's you? You are her Valentine stalker?" He asks in disbelief. "No fucking way."

"I'm not a stalker, just a man with a crush. I was trying to be fucking romantic. She thought I was a stalker?"

"I did. I've been walking her to her car every damn night this week. I thought some wack-job wanted her dead. The blood, the creepy letters, the black roses—it was creepy. Now that I know it is you, it makes sense. Dude, you fucking suck at romance."

Offended, I give him the bird. "Fuck off, man. I am trying. I used lyrics to her favorite songs. I got gifts I knew she would love. I wanted to show I know her. I want to be with her. I'm in love with her."

His eyes widened in surprise. "I didn't know you cared that much about Waverly. I knew you had a crush but love?"

"How could I not? She is perfect in every way possible. Spending time with her over the past three years, the crush changed into love."

"Wow," he states, looking lost in thought.

"Yea."

We stand in awkward silence for a minute.

"She loved the other gifts, though. I found her twirling in the lobby holding her books," Ren informs me. "Ranting and raving about them, actually. I couldn't get her to shut up."

"Really?"

"Yep," Ren proclaims. "Enough sappy shit. Let's order pizza and drink beer."

I agree. "Let me get this off my dick and put on pants. You order the pizza. Beer is in the fridge."

"Fuck, man, please put the one-eyes monster away," he

laughs until tears roll down his face. "Fuck me. You're never living this down, Tripod."

I go to my bathroom and remove my soft dick from the mold. It is fucked up. *Damn it!* Good thing I bought extra silicone just in case. I figured if I needed to purchase more for my size, and that I would no doubt fuck it up once and purchased more. I will try again after Ren goes home.

Ren stayed for about two hours. We ate pizza, drank a couple of beers, and played video games. When he left, he made joking comments about me and my *Cockolate*. But I noticed he took his home. I shook my head and laughed.

The second time worked like a charm. I finished the mold, melted the chocolate, and poured it into the mold. I placed it in the fridge while I crafted the letter to go with it.

COCKOLATE?

WAVERLY

It's my day off, but I've to do the tattoo for Coben, I mean Tripod. I don't have to go in until around two to get everything set up.

Though I chugged the caffeine earlier, I feel jumpier than usual. The first letter from my stalker or crush or whatever said by Valentine's Day; I'd be his.

Well, today is Valentine's Day.

Will I receive a letter, gift, or finally, he'll make an appearance? I haven't been this nervous since I was doing my first tattoo on an actual person.

To keep busy, avoiding the thoughts fluttering in and out of my head like pestering flies, I cleaned my house, and I did my laundry. *Yep, I even folded it and put it away!* Unfortunately, this didn't require too much time. Living alone, I keep it relatively clean. When I finished, it is only noon. I decided to shower, dress, have a quick lunch, and head to the shop early.

I walk in. The jingle of the damn bell gives me a start. I flip the bird and chuckle at myself. If I didn't laugh, I might burst into tears from the anxiety. Maybe I should have called the police from the beginning, and I wouldn't be in this predicament.

Behind the counter, Ren says, "Hey, Waverly. I wasn't expecting you yet."

"Bored at home. I decided to get ready for Tripod." When I mention Tripod, Ren bites his lip, near laughing. "What?"

"Nothing," he says, but not looking at me. "You got this in the mail today."

"Okay—"

The door jingles interrupting my interrogation of his strange behavior. I take the package and squeak. My new tattoo machine is finally here.

"Hey, James. Come on back, I'm ready for you," Ren says to his client.

"Are you going to be here to walk me to my car tonight?"

"Nope. This is my last appointment. Tripod can walk you to your car," he smirks. The glint in his eye looks like trouble.

"Alright, well, have a good session," I reply, confused as fuck.

To calm my nerves, I grab chamomile tea from our cupboard and put it in my cup. I can't do a tattoo with shaky hands. I sip my tea and slowly relax. Knowing that I am at work and Ren is in the other room helps too.

Excitement vibrates under the surface. I'm ready to use my new machine. Bonus, using it on Tripod's body—well, the thought makes my body vibrate in a different way.

Three o'clock on the dot, Tripod arrives. The man has never been late. I almost wonder if he has Obsessive Compulsive Disorder.

"Hey, Waverly."

"Hey, Tripod," I smile at him.

"Coben. That damn nickname is forever going to haunt me," he sighs.

"Sorry, no can do, I already told you that," I say, throwing a wink his way.

I understand he's getting a tattoo, and a person wants to be comfortable, but I wonder if he ever wears jeans. Today, he's dressed in gray sweatpants and sporting a shirt from his favorite hockey team. The sweatpants are tighter, maybe joggers? *Is that the name?* I flush at the thought of him jogging and his dick swinging back and forth. I almost drool.

Shaking my head, I notice he has a red rectangle gift box in his hands. "What is that?"

"Oh, this?" He glances down. "This is for you."

That is weird. I already received my new machine, and I am not expecting anything else. He hands it to me, and sure enough, it has my name neatly written on the envelope attached to the top of the box. My heart drops when I see the writing matches the stalker gifts. I make sure to school my features. I don't want to alarm Tripod or Ren.

"Follow me so we can get you tatted up," I say, putting a little extra sway in my hips as I walk, knowing he is behind me.

In my room, I sit the wrapped gift on my counter and try to ignore it. I start getting the tattoo stencil ready to transfer the drawing onto Tripod's chest.

"Take off your shirt," I say, spinning my chair to him.

"Done," he grins. "Aren't you going to open your gift?" He gestures to the box.

"No. I have a tattoo to do."

"I think you should open it."

Frowning, I glance between him and the box. "Will it make you happy if I open it?"

"Yes, it would."

I grab the note and rip it open. When I slip out the paper, I'm relieved to find no blood. The words are weird. My crush can't even spell chocolate.

Waverly,

> Today is the day. I will make you mine. I'm tired of waiting. I would like to wine and dine you. But first, here is a special gift. I hope it causes you to shift and not become miffed. Please enjoy this one of a kind, limited edition, Cockolate. Do not use it to copulate.
>
> Love,
Your Valentine Crush

Miffed? Copulate? Who the hell uses these words? I use a box cutter to slice the paper. Inhaling a deep breath, I peel back the sides and peeking inside. The gift is wrapped in a wine bottle-shaped bag and has tissue paper in it. I lift the bag, but the handle breaks from the weight of the gift.

I sit the box on the floor and use both hands to lift the gift bag out of the box. I try to peer inside to make sure it isn't going to harm Tripod or me. All I see is something brown wrapped in... *Is that saran wrap?* I carefully take the red and pink gift tissue out of the bag. What I'm left with is—

Confused, I turn my chair away from Tripod. I pull out a huge, solid, milk chocolate cock. I shove it in the bag and burst out laughing. I'm not sure why I'm laughing. It could be from fear, embarrassment, or from the absurdity of having a solid chocolate dong in a bag. My crush sure has a sense of humor or is super fucking sleazy.

"Well?" Tripod questions.

I grab the chocolate *cockasaurus* out of the bag and lift it for him to see. It will be forever known as the *cockasaurus*—this thing is enormous. I say the first thing to pop into my head. "Thank god it doesn't have pubes, or I would have thought it was an actual fucking mold."

"I shave," Tripod whispers.

"Good to know, Tripod. I'm so glad you don't have girls flossing with your pubes," I laugh even harder, picturing some chick flossing with pubes during a blowjob. I bring the offending enormous chocolate erection up to my arm to show a comparison. "This thing is as big as my forearm."

"Wanna compare with the real thing?" Tripod asks.

"Wait; what?" The fit of giggles dies. I study his face, realizing he's serious. "What are you saying?"

"I shave. And if you want to compare the real thing to your forearm, here it is." He gestures towards his now semi-erect penis.

My eyes flick to his groin. "You're joking, right? If you're saying this is a *real* mold of your dick, that means—" He nods his head *yes*. "You're my fucking stalker?"

"Valentine cru—" he tries to correct.

"Hold the fuck up," I interrupt him. "You mean to fucking say instead of just telling me you fucking like me, you give left weird-ass gifts? For weeks, I thought I had a stalker!" I yell the last part. "Who the fuck even does that?"

"I swear, I realize you misunderstood. Honest. I didn't know until Ren walked in on me making a Cockolate for you."

My mouth opens, then closes, then opens again. "I want to laugh at your awkward moment. And at the fact, it is called a Cockolate, but I am too damn pissed. You put *fake blood* in a fucking letter."

"Yes, but—" He tries to explain, but I forge on.

"You sent me black fucking roses in a damn vase that looked like a goddamn urn. You sent me my favorite fucking things in a big box. Yes, all of the stuff was sweet, but it is fucking creepy you know me that well. When I don't know much about you. Then—then to fucking top it all off, you give me a solid chocolate mold of your cock." I take a deep breath and pause.

Leaning up in the chair, Tripod resembles a whipped dog. "Waverly, you have to listen to me. I have an explanation for everything," he pleads.

"I don't have to do shit. I need you to leave Coben. I can't. I don't know what the fuck this even means." My head falls into my hands.

He rubs his hands on his sweats. "I wanted to tell you it was me. I thought you enjoyed everything. Every time I walked in after a gift, you looked flushed and happy."

"Because you walked in looking sexy as fuck." I slap a hand over my mouth.

"You think I'm sexy?"

Right now, really, is this important? "Yes, Coben. Who the hell wouldn't? But that is beside the point. I need you to leave. You can have Ren do this tattoo if you want."

"I'll wait until you are ready, or I won't get it at all."

"That is your choice, Tripod. You need to leave."

"Fine. I get it. When you're ready to talk this through, give me a call," he turns and walks out while throwing his shirt on.

I watched out of the window as Tripod walked with his head down and hand on his heart. The whole situation was fucked. Tripod, my stalker, crush, whatever? *Damn! Maybe I should have let him explain, but he went about it wrong.*

He professed his love in every letter. He showed his love with every damn gift. I'm not ready to be loved like that yet. I haven't been hurt in the past or anything cliché. I just...I need time to think.

While locking the shop up, I text Laken and ask her to stop at my house. She agrees. I walk to my car, paying close attention to my surroundings out of habit.

When I pull into my driveway, I grab my confectionary gut buster 3000 and take it in the house. It was too pretty to throw away. I stick it in the refrigerator. I call into our favorite Chinese restaurant and order our favorites to be delivered.

Thirty minutes later, the food arrives at the same time as Laken walks in.

"What's wrong?" She immediately asks.

"Why would you think something is wrong?"

"Girl. You ordered our favorite comfort foods. We only order this amount of food when we are eating our feelings," she says, digging through the bags.

"Coben."

"Who?" she asks in confusion.

"Tripod. Coben is his real name. Tripod is a nickname." *Which is obvious, I suppose. Who would name their child Tripod?*

"What about him?"

I walk over to the refrigerator and get the gift bag. I pull out the Cockolate and set it on my table.

Laken stares in disbelief. Then she starts guffawing. "He bought you a huge chocolate weiner?"

"It is a Cockolate, and it is a fucking mold of his cock."

Her eyes widened in surprise. "Girl, you're lying."

"Not according to him. Before I knew it was his anaconda, I made a joke. I said it was the same size as my forearm. He asked if I wanted to try it against the real thing."

She raises her hands. "So why the fuck are you not with him riding that womb raider? Why the hell are we eating Chinese instead of you being pounded into the fucking headboard until you have a concussion?"

For the next hour, I tell her about the gifts, being afraid of a stalker, and then feeling betrayed when I found out it was him.

"Let me get this straight. You've got a hot man sending you gifts, most of which you fucking loved. Everything to show you he loved you. Or rather cares for you, since I know you're allergic to the *L-word*."

"I'm not allergic to love," I defend.

"Yes, you are. In each of your relationships, your partner leaves because they wanted more, and you wouldn't take the next step."

"What? No, they were all mutual breakups."

"You may believe that, but the relationships fizzle out because you hold back." She chews on a dumpling.

"I don't," I reply and wonder. "Do I?"

"That is probably why you freaked out on Tripod; I mean Coben."

"And I barely know him," I insist.

She waves chopsticks in the air. "Girl, you've talked about the man for years. I don't believe you. Tell me what you know about him."

"He is a photographer. He loves tattoos. He also likes Lil' Wayne. Most of his older tattoos he got in college, being a practice canvas for Ren. That's why he comes in so often to get them covered up on the house. Oh, and he loves wearing basketball shorts and gray sweatpants," I smile, thinking about him.

"Sounds like you know him pretty damn well. Does he have any pets?" she asks while petting Koopa.

"No. He loves animals but hates cleaning up the hair."

"See. You freaked out for no damn reason."

"I only know those things because he comes to the shop so much. He got his nickname in college, and it goes with his career. I know he loves tattoos because he comes so often. I say he likes Lil' Wayne because it's his ringtone. I assume he likes wearing those clothes because that's all I see him in," I defend.

"I'm not sure why you're arguing with me. You didn't have to think too hard. You gave me those things off the top of your head." Laken stares at me. "You know him."

Stubborn, I reply, "Maybe."

"Let the dust settle and hear him out. Do the man's tattoo. Give him my appointment tomorrow."

"No, it is for your other special tattoo. I can call him."

She put her hand on mine. "Don't fight me. I'm not feeling a tattoo right now."

"Are you okay?"

"I will be. Eventually, Preston and I are done for good. I won't go back to him."

"Maybe you should talk to Ren and apologize for ghosting him," I hint.

"I will when he talks to me and lets me explain. I'll wait for the relationship and not the hook-up. I need a bit before I jump headfirst into any connection."

I squeeze her hand. "You know I'm here for you whenever you need me."

"Same to you. We have to keep each other from ruining our lives." She hugs me.

Laken's phone vibrates, and she picks it up. Her voice sounds cheery and hopeful. I have no idea who it is. I make my way to the kitchen and grab a bottle of wine and two glasses. She comes back in and says it was a friend. I shrug and get comfy on the couch with our wine. We turn on some mindless TV show, and I think about Tripod and everything that has transpired.

FUCKED IT UP

COBEN

I left the tattoo shop as Waverly asked. My chest hurts. I rubbed it all the way to the car with my head hanging in defeat. I never wanted to hurt her. My actions were romantic, unique, but I guess I took things a little too far.

Instead of going home, I go to my local bar. I sit, throwing back shots of Jack. I texted Ren to join me. I'm hoping he has advice. He is going to want to kill me for hurting Waverly.

"Hey buddy, how about we slow down on the shots," Ren says, startling me.

"Nah, I fuckin' need 'em," I slur slightly.

"No, you don't. We are going to talk about this."

"What is there really to talk about? I fucked it up. I fucked it up so bad she kicked me out of the tattoo shop."

"Damn. I don't think I have ever seen Waverly mad before. How did you tell her it was you?"

It hurts, but I tell him everything—even the part about the pubes.

"That is how you fucking told her? Seriously?" Ren asks, shaking his head and laughing.

"What is wrong with the way I did it? She was laughing until she realized I was serious."

"Did you just hear yourself? *She was laughing until she realized I was serious,*" Ren mocked in a deep voice. "She thought you were joking. Do you not see the flaw in your execution?"

"Now that you mention it," I say, "I could have done it better."

"Could have? How about, you should have. What you should have done is told her you were her crush before you gave her a solid chocolate cock."

"Cockolate," I inform him.

"How much have you had to drink? Are you seriously worried about the name of the *chococock*? I'm more worried about you and Waverly. Was she crying?" he asks, his voice laced in worry.

"No, more like fumin'. Steam coming out of her ears." I try using my hands by my ears to demonstrate.

"Good thing she wasn't crying. I would have had to kick your ass. I'm going to call Laken really quick and see if she has an update on Waverly."

"Tell her I'm sorry," I yell at him as he walks away.

He waves a hand in acknowledgment. I turn around and slam back another shot and throw my signal to the bartender. He drops off another shot, and I ask for two beers on tap.

"Okay, I'm back. The good news is Laken is with her. She wants you to take her appointment tomorrow at twelve o'clock. So let's finish this beer, pay the tab, and I will drive you home in your truck."

I hiccup. "Waverly still wants to talk to me?"

"Yes. That is what Laken said."

The gears in my head turn slow, addled by liquor. "Or is this a trap to get us to talk? I don't want to upset Waverly. I want her to *want* to talk to me, to love me, *to want to be with me*."

"I know, buddy. Let's get this beer drunk so that I can get you home. Laken assured me that she wants you there. No more worrying, just enjoy the buzz."

I chug the glass of beer and slam the shot back. I throw $200 on the bar. I go to stand up but stumble back into my seat. "Fucked up again," I mumble.

"Yep, you got fucked up, that is for sure," Ren laughs. "Is this enough to pay his tab?"

The bartender must say yes because we get up to leave. Ren lifts me and slings my arm around his shoulders. Together we get out of the bar and into the chilly night. He drives me home, unlocks my door, and I face plant into bed.

♡

I WAKE up to my mouth full of sand and a monster of a headache. I should not have drunk whiskey. No more drinking the pain away.

I get my ass out of bed, shower, brush my gritty teeth, and eat toast. I hope the toast soaks up some of the liquor so I can eat more before my tattoo. I lay in the dark, cool bedroom until an hour before my appointment. I fix myself a plain turkey sandwich and head out the door.

Feeling like garbage, I stop for coffee. I get Waverly's favorite, and I go for a black coffee. I arrive a little earlier than my appointment but head inside anyway.

"Welcome to Tatted Canvas," Waverly greets and then fumbles, seeing it's me. "Oh, hey, Coben. Come on back."

I'm ecstatic to hear my name on her lips. Not Tripod, but Coben. Also a little worried. What if I fucked up our friendship? Waves of desire dance to my cock. *Now is not the time for you to salute her.* I follow her back and close the door. "I brought you a coffee."

"Thank you." She accepts the cup. "I totally need it today."

"Me too. I drank a little too much last night."

"Same. Wine hangovers are the worst."

"Whiskey is pretty rough too." We smile awkwardly at each other. My heart skips a beat at her beauty.

"So before we get to your tattoo, we need to talk. It was cute, your gifts, but super creepy." She sighs and grips the cup in her hand. "I know I blew up yesterday, and for that, I do apologize. Please start explaining so we can work this out. I don't want any weirdness between us."

Relief, and worry, hit my gut. It's a strange mix of feelings. "I am ready to explain and ask for your forgiveness."

"Forgiveness isn't needed. I overreacted. I can tell a lot of thought went into the gifts and letters. I should have heard you out."

Taking a deep breath, I launch into my explanation. "For the bloody Valentine, I researched all of your favorite bands' songs and strategically picked the lyrics that I felt truly represented my feelings for you. The fake blood was just a pun I was hoping you would understand and appreciate."

"Okay," she interrupts me. "I like the effort. But the blood was creepy. If I wasn't a tattoo artist and knew fake blood from the real thing, you could be in jail for stalking. Keep that in mind for future romantic ideas later in life."

"I see that now. I truly thought you enjoyed all the gifts. The way you appeared afterward, it made me feel like I was doing the right things," I sincerely proclaim.

"As I said, you're the reason I was looking at you, not the gifts."

I can't help it; I smile. "You think I'm sexy?"

"Seriously. Is that the only thing you fucking heard before I kicked you out?"

"And the part where you compared my cock size to your forearm." I grin when she rolls her eyes. It feels good to joke with her. It provides a modicum of hope.

"You are foul, sir."

"I know. And you like it."

"That is true."

I explain the flowers, the meaning of the roses. We discuss how black roses not only mean death and mourning but also represent new things, significant change, hope, and courage. When she remarks I have brains with looks, I can't help but glow.

"I wanted you to know that we're meant to be together. I don't want to be just friends. I want more."

She fiddles with the lid on her coffee. "I'm not sure if we're meant to be together. That is moving too fast, Coben."

"This isn't just some little crush. I am truly interested in seeing where this goes." My hand itches to grab her hand, to feel her touch, but I've already fucked up enough. "The Cockolate. The way you looked at me in my sweatpants and gym shorts, well, I thought of a Clone-A-Willy. While shopping, I saw the limited edition Cockolate. At the time, I thought it was funny and sexy. No real research into that one."

"The *cockasaurus* may be in my fridge." A pink blush covers her cheeks.

"*Cockasaurus?*"

"It's what I call it," she snickers, hiding her face.

Humor is good. I can work with humor. "I'm not sure how you feel about everything. But I want to try us."

"Try us? Like, have sex?"

"Date, have sex, get married, whatever happens. I want to be more than friends." My voice is rough with emotions. "I'd love it if you would give me a try."

She starts laughing. My heart drops. *I came on too strong. Fuck. I knew I would fuck this up.*

"Sorry. It's not you, I swear," Waverly states, wiping at her eyes.

"Are you breaking up with me before we even go on our first date?" I give a nervous chuckle. "Isn't that the excuse everyone gives when they want to break up?"

"No! It's just...when you said give me a try. Laken gave me similar advice." Mimicking her friend, throwing her hair over her shoulder to exaggerate the pantomime, Waverly says, "*So why the fuck are you not with him riding that womb raider? Why the hell are we eating Chinese instead of you being pounded into the fucking headboard until you have a concussion?*" She doubles over, holding her stomach as fits of laughter hit again.

I like how Laken thinks.

When she calms down, Waverly smiles. She is alight with humor. "I say we give this a try. Maybe a date and see where this goes."

"Sounds perfect, Waverly," I agree, heart pounding.

"We can figure out the details, but we should start your tattoo. Take off your clothes. I...I...mean your shirt," she stumbles on her words.

"Be careful what you wish for. I can be naked in two seconds."

"Two seconds?" A skeptical eyebrow shoots up. " Damn, that's fast."

"Doesn't take long when you aren't wearing much."

She flushes at my words. Clearing her throat, Waverly mumbles something about getting her stuff ready. She taps the foot peddle of her gun. An hour and a half later, she adds the last touches to the chest piece.

Thank god. I don't know how much more I can handle. Her hands upon my body have my little soldier ready to fire. My nipples have never been sensitive, but as soon as she touched them, my cock jumped to attention. I've had to control my breathing the whole session. It was a challenge not to moan.

"Finished," she declares in a proud tone.

I blow out a large breath and try to calm my rapid heartbeat. I stand, go to the full-length mirror on the wall, and blink. Waverly transformed my one-dimensional skull tattoo into artwork.

Waverly added layers of dimension into the skull by using reds, pinks, blacks, whites, and grays to make the skulls and flowers look like they're about to pop out of my skin. The shading is perfect, the lines precise. Nothing but perfection.

"Do you not like it?" She asks in an unsure voice.

"I love it." *I love you. I want to say that, but I refrain.* "It is perfect. Thank you."

"No problem." She cleans up her work area, and I follow her to the shop's front to pay.

"That will be eighty bucks."

"It costs more than that," I state.

She cocks a grin at me. "I gave you *the friend* discount,"

"I don't want *the friend* discount. I want to pay you the right price. You deserve it," I argue.

"Fine. Eighty dollars, sir. I'm giving you *the boyfriend* discount. It is only fair since you paid for the inks I used. Don't argue, or I'll cancel our date tomorrow."

"I'm your boyfriend?" I ask. "Wait. Did you say date?"

"Yes, sir."

Did I say something and forget when I tried to keep my little soldier under control? Damn! "When did this happen? When do I pick you up?" My brain overloads with excitement.

"Well, while I tattooing, I thought of your romantic gestures.

Even though it was sorta botched, the reasoning behind everything pretty much melted my heart. I decided we can try the boyfriend and girlfriend gig. See where it goes, you know?"

Fuck yes! "And the date tomorrow? What are we doing? Where are we going? Do you like sushi?"

"Calm down, Tripod. Pick me up; we'll grab some greasy, delicious food from somewhere and then have drinks at my house or yours. Whatever you choose."

"No more Tripod," I say, moving around the counter and backing her against it.

"Coben," she whispers.

"Fuck." I lean close to her ear. "Hearing my name come from your delectable mouth makes me rock hard. Use only my real name."

"Or what? Are you gonna spank me?" she asks breathlessly.

I go to reply when the damn bell jingles.

"Get a fucking room, you two. You're gonna scare away the clients," Ren jokes.

"We'll finish this conversation tomorrow. And the answer is yes; I will spank you. I will grab you by your hair, tugging it just enough to feel the pain. Then I will pull your pants down, bend you over my lap and turn that juicy ass of yours bright red," I whisper in her ear.

She moans against my neck while grabbing my shirt and trying to keep me close to her. I pull away but sneak a quick kiss on her cheek.

"See ya tomorrow, Peaches."

"Peaches?" she asks in confusion.

"It's what I imagine you taste like," I growl.

She mouths, *Fuck*.

"Text me your address and time." I turn and say, "See ya, Ren."

"See ya. No more making out on the counter. Don't want

your spunk all over the place," Ren chortles, flipping through a catalog.

I flip him the bird and head out of the shop. I go home to clean the hell out of my whole house, hoping to bring Waverly here tomorrow.

DATE NIGHT

WAVERLY

Trying to pick an outfit out to wear for a date is stressful as hell. I texted Laken ten minutes ago to come over and help. She assured me she would be here in the next half an hour. I bite my nails and sort through my closet like it will give me all the answers to life. *Wouldn't it be great if it could?*

I must have zoned out because Laken comes strolling in the room and drops her purse onto my bed.

"I brought makeup so I can help you get ready. I'm so excited you gave Tripod a chance."

"How could I not when he explained everything. Almost every gift had a fucking deep and meaningful reason behind it," I say dreamily.

"Tell me what he said while I dig through your closet. Do you have any garters and thigh highs?"

"In there," I point towards a dresser drawer. I tell her a watered-down version. Meanwhile, she digs deep into my closet. Finally, she comes out with a big grin and a barely-there dress.

"This is the one," she says in triumph. My black mini dress

with lace sleeves that hang off the shoulders hangs in her hand. She paired it with my black fishnet thigh highs and black garter belt. She dives back in, for what I assume is a hunt for shoes.

"Are you planning on me getting laid?" I ask, holding up the fishnets and garter. "Do I not get any panties?"

"You're going to get laid. No panties. You can't have a panty line. Why would you not jump his bones? You have seen a mold of his cock. What do you call it again?"

"*Cockasaurus*, chocolate dong, confectionary gut buster 3000, Cockolate…" I tick off each nickname I think I have used since getting the damn thing.

"What the fuck? Confectionary gut buster 3000? Oh my god. That is gold."

"Humor is my way of dealing with life when it gets hard. And that chocolate is hard." We burst out laughing.

"Here we are," She says, slithering out of the closet with a pair of red strappy caged heels.

She motions for me to get dressed, and I do. When I'm done, Laken whistles.

"He is going to want to shag you. Yeah, baby, yeah," she mocks in a terrible Austin Powers impression, that makes me giggle. I appreciate it. My nerves calm a smidgen.

I feel like a teenager getting ready for prom. She straightens and teases my hair to give it lots of volume. Once done, she moves on to makeup. Against my usual smokey eye and black lipstick, she chooses a natural look—soft, rose-gold shadow fading to peach, apricot blush on my cheeks, and a simple brown eyeliner.

"Don't give me that look, Waverly. You can still wear black lipstick," she says. She digs in her purse and comes out with a new black lipstick. "This is supposed to be life-proof lipstick. I got it, so you don't leave a black ring around his dick when you are sucking it." She wiggles her brows.

"Laken!" I shriek. "It's our first date. I'm not doing that yet," I say in an unconvincing tone.

"*Buuullll-ssshhhiiiittt*," she sing-songs. "Put it on and shut up." Phe picks up her purse and kisses me on the cheek. "Have fun and text me when you get home. Tomorrow."

"I'm not staying the night," I argue.

"Yeah, okay," she says sarcastically. Then she is out the door but not before I hear her say to go on in, to Coben.

"Waverly?" I hear Coben call out.

"I'm almost ready. I'll be out in a minute. Make yourself at home."

I take a steadying breath while looking in the mirror, adjusting my dress, and fluffing my hair. I swipe on the life-proof lipstick and then test it on the back of my hand. Wow, it really does work. Is it dick sucking proof?

Jeez, Laken implanted the image in my head, and now I can't stop thinking about it.

Shaking the naughty thoughts out of my head, I leave my bedroom and go to the living room to greet my date. As I turn the corner, my breath leaves my body. He looks gorgeous as hell. He is in a black leather jacket paired with dark blue jeans and a black button-up shirt. Drool-worthy. He sits on my loveseat, caressing Koopa. I'm thoroughly surprised the cat lets Coben touch him. He only allows me to love him.

"Fuck me. You look hot."

"Maybe, I will. Let's see if you can be a good boy," I tease, biting my lip.

He groans and says, "We'll never get through dinner if you keep talking like that."

"Maybe I'm not hungry," I say with a lifted brow.

"Waverly. I cooked a meal. We're going to my house, eating dinner, and sharing conversation," he replies sternly.

I bat my lashes at him. "So, no sex?"

"I didn't ask you out to get you into bed," he defends. "I'm not opposed to it, but that isn't the reason."

"Relax, I was joking. I wanted to see if I could tease you." I squeeze his shoulder. "Did you say you cooked for me? That is sweet. Let's go; I am hungry."

We walk down to his truck, and he opens the door. Chivalry isn't dead. He leans over me and buckles my seatbelt. So close, his scent invades, making my knees tremble. Thank goodness I am already seated, or they would have buckled. I admit it was hard not to sniff him while he sat in my tattoo chair. Hell, it was hard not to lick every inch of his delicious body.

The drive is short. We live ten minutes away from each other. I go to open my truck door, but Coben stops me. "I've got it," he says.

"Coben, I can open my own door."

"I know you can, but my momma taught me to be a gentleman. If I didn't open your door and she heard about it, I would be in deep shit."

The way he says it, I believe him. "Are you sure you aren't doing it so you can look at my ass?" I joke.

"Well, no harm in taking advantage of a good situation," he winks. Coben rushes out of the truck and around the front to open my door. I thank him as we walk up to his front door. When we walk inside, my mouth drops open in awe. His open floor plan is gorgeous.

"This is *mi casa*," he states, dropping keys in a dish by the door.

"Lovely design. Great lines, and clean. Minimalist, which I love. What is that delicious smell?" I ask, sniffing the air.

"That would be dinner." He puts a warm palm to the middle of my back, directing me to the dining table. "I made bacon-wrapped asparagus, baked lobster tails, garlic butter steaks on the grill, and a molten chocolate lava cake for dessert."

"Wow! You can cook?" I ask in amazement.

"Yes, I can. My momma taught me to cook when I was younger. She didn't want me to rely on my future wife to make dinner or rely on fast food. She said women love when their men can cook them a meal," he shrugs with a smirk.

"Sounds like momma is a damn good woman."

"She is. Do you want a tour first or food?"

I think about my options for a moment. *If I do a tour first, we may end up in his bed, and dinner would get cold. Let's face it. This man fixed a romantic dinner for us. My panties are drenched. Wait, I'm not wearing panties. Anyway, if we eat first, I may be too full for sex later.*

"Dinner?" *Damn, my stomach won.*

"Have a seat, and I will bring the food in," he laughs at my questioning answer.

I do as I am told, thinking he will set the table and bring the food in the dining room on platters. Nope, This sexy man made my plate for me. He piled it up with a little bit of everything.

"Oh my! You didn't have to make my pate. I could have done it. Thank you so much. I am getting the queen treatment. I could get used to this."

"You will get used to it. I promise you that."

We eat and chat. I enjoy casual conversation and food. Coben's favorite color is red, and his favorite snack is white cheddar cheese crackers. He is an only child and a self-declared momma's boy.

My story is boring. I tell him about my step-brother, who is seven years my senior. My mom remarried when I was thirteen. By the time they married, my stepbrother Marcus was twenty. We aren't close.

When we finish dinner, I offer to wash the dishes, but Coben refuses. He insists he'll toss them in the dishwasher later. We move to the living room with wine.

"So?"

"Yea?" I ask.

"Why is this awkward? It shouldn't be awkward. We know each other. Hell, we had a great conversation during dinner."

Shut up, brain. Don't say it. Don't say it! "Maybe it's because all we want to do is jump each other's bones, and you are trying hard to be a gentleman?" *Shit. I said it.*

"Waverly. I just wanted a nice date with you," he defends as if I'm accusing him of something terrible.

"Coben," I mock. "What if I did plan it? Maybe I am wearing life-proof lipstick." I wipe my lips with the back of my hand to show him. "Maybe I have been eye-fucking you just as long as you have been eye-fucking me. Maybe I am dressed specifically for it."

"Life-proof lipstick?"

"You have a one-track mind. Life-proof means you can eat, drink, and wear it all day, and it won't come off."

"Wow," he says.

"Maybe we should see if it is truly life-proof." I offer him my hand. "Or we can sit here and chat. You with your boner. I'll manage with my drenched thighs."

Fuck.

I hear him mutter under his breath. I cross my legs, causing my dress to rise to show my garter and stockings. His eyes immediately hone in on the movement. I flip my hair back and give my sexiest smile.

I can see the war raging in his head. His face shows every emotion. Finally, he looks up, and his amber eyes dilated to the point they appear black. He is breathing heavily as if he is a bull ready to charge. He aggressively runs his hands through his hair.

Tired of waiting for Coben to choose, I lower myself to the floor and push him into a relaxed position on the couch. I reach for the button on his jeans, but he grabs my hands. The look on his face is one of longing mixed with desire.

"If you do that, I will not last."

"You can return the favor while you recover." I lick my lips.

"I love the way you think," he says while letting go of my hands.

Reaching up, I gather my hair and secure it with an elastic. "Remove your pants and underwear," I demand.

Coben stands up and drops his pants. "I would love to listen about the underwear, but I go commando," he says with a shrug.

I whimper at the sight of his nakedness. I try to scissor my legs to relieve some of the pressure, but it makes it worse. "Shirt too," I squeak out.

He doesn't hesitate. "What next?"

"Sit back and relax," I suggest. I go to get into place and then change my mind. He deserves a little show. I carefully remove my arms out of the lace sleeves and pull the dress over my head. I tried to do it in a sexy way, but it didn't work out.

Coben sucks in a breath at the sight of my bare chest. "Christ almighty. You are fucking perfect."

Pleased, I lower myself to my knees. I moisten my lips and palm his erection. I can't even close my hand around the damn thing. I can, in fact, now prove that the Cockolate was a mold of the real thing. *Fucking cockasuarus is an appropriate name for something about to destroy my insides most deliciously.*

My hand glides up and down a few times, testing my grip and seeing what Coben likes. I add my other hand twisting on the downstroke. I take one hand off his shaft and cradle his balls. I roll them in my hand.

"Waverly, please," he pleads.

"Please what?"

"Please put your mouth on me."

Something stops me. I want the dominant man, saying he'll

spank me. I continue lightly caressing and fondling. He holdings back. I take it a step further by leaning forward and lightly lick before backing away.

Finally, after a few light licks, he grabs my ponytail and stops me. He pulls my hair, making me look at him, and says, "I was trying to be a gentleman, but you've pushed me too far, Waverly."

"Good. I don't need a gentleman. I want *Tripod* to come out and play," I goad him.

"I told you what would happen if you called me that again. I will dish out your punishment later," his voice dropped octaves with lust. "Now, you are going to suck my cock."

I moan as he stands and rests the tip of his dick on my lips. I try to stick out my tongue to taste the pre-come, but he pulls away before I can.

"Not until I say so."

I shake my head, prepared to do whatever he says. He again places the head of his cock on my lips and waits. "Open." I do as he says, and he finally pushes his beautiful cock in my mouth. "Relax, I won't hurt you. Here, put your hands on my thighs. Squeeze when you need a break."

I didn't realize I tensed up. I place my hands on Coben's muscled thighs and relax. As soon as he gets to the back of my throat, I swallow out of habit. "Do that again." I do it two more times. "You're going to have to stop, or I'm going to come." With that, I double my efforts, moving his cock farther down my throat and swallowing. He throbs and releases his hot milky come into my throat. I continue swallowing, enjoying every moment.

He pulls out of my mouth, scoops me up off the floor, and carries me to his bedroom. I tense up, prepared for him to throw me on the bed. Instead, he sits down. Careful, he maneuvers me to my stomach, and I'm draped over his lap. "So what was it that you called me?"

"Tripod."

"Are you supposed to call me that?"

"Only if I want to be spanked?"

He laughs. "These fucking stockings and garter are so fucking hot. And no panties? Are you trying to give a man a heart attack?" he asks while rubbing my ass. He dips his fingers between my thighs. "So fucking wet. You're dripping onto my lap. Did you like sucking my cock?"

"Yes," I hiss. His touch sears. I feel like I could combust if he put pressure on my clit.

He slowly brings his hand back up and continues rubbing. "You have one nice juicy ass, Peaches," he tells me in a voice of admiration.

"Thank you, Tripod," I say, glancing over my shoulder, smirking.

Whack! His hand moved so fast I didn't have time to flinch. The sting is sharp but quickly morphs into the dark pleasure I love. *Whack!* He lands another smack on the other cheek. I whimper.

"More."

"My Peaches loves pain."

He doesn't leave me wanting. He rains down smack after smack. By the time he quits, I'm floating from desire. Coben stands with me and gently lays me on the bed, and sweetly kisses me.

I spread my legs to make space for him between my thighs. I deepen the kiss and grind up against his length sitting at my entrance, hoping it will slip inside. He breaks our kiss, continuing light kisses down my jaw, over to my ear, and down my neck, leading to my right breast.

Taking a nipple between his teeth, he bites down and swipes

his tongue back and forth until I am squirming and grabbing his head to push my breast further into his mouth. He sucks it deep into his mouth and lets it go with a pop. He kisses over to the other breast and repeats the process.

Coben turned me into a big ball of pleasure with a few smacks on my ass and kisses. *If this is heaven, I never want to leave.*

One last suck, then he releases the other nipple and licks his way down towards my mons. He slows at my belly button, teasing it with light licks and nips.

"Please."

"Please what? Tell me what you want, Peaches."

"Coben. Stop fucking teasing me and eat my pussy."

"Yes, ma'am." He stops teasing immediately. I've never censored myself, and I'm not about to start now. He clamps his mouth around my clit, sucking and nibbling. I go off like a bomb, yelling out his name. He moves his mouth down to my opening and drinks in my essence.

I have never gotten off so quickly in my life. I try to push his head away from me, but he won't let up. When he does, he is predatory and feral.

Licking his lips, he prowls up my body. "I knew you would taste like peaches and cream'"

He kisses me again. I taste myself on his lips, and my libido sparks back to life in an instant. I run my hands up and down his body, mapping his muscles with my fingertips.

We get hot and heavy again. Grinding, touching, tasting, anywhere, and everywhere we can. A few more grinding motions, and Coben's cock slides home in one smooth thrust. I pant out in pain and pleasure. He is enormous yet perfect.

It is as if two puzzle pieces are connected. "Fuck, you feel so good," I manage between breaths.

"You were made for me. Your pussy was like a beacon for my

cock." Thrusting in and out, he hits a spot that causes quivers of delight. He lifts my leg, placing it on his shoulder, and flips me sideways.

Coben continues thrusting into me until I start to shake. My walls clamp down on his cock, and I shout his name. A few more thrusts, and his cock is jolting and shooting his hot seed inside me.

He pulls out too late. "Shit. I forgot a condom. And I pulled out too late. Fuck." He gets up, somewhat panicked.

"I guess Cardi B had it right."

"What?" He asks in utter confusion.

"She said, *wet-ass pussy make that pullout game weak*."

He bursts out laughing. Laughing so hard he has to hold his stomach, and he falls on the bed. "Did you really just quote a Cardi B after I came inside you?"

"I deal with fear with jokes. It is my way of coping," I shrug.

"I love that about you."

"I know."

"Okay, smartass. I'll be there for you if you're pregnant though you know that, right?"

"You better be since you're my boyfriend," I threaten.

"I will. I'm so sorry." He covers his face and heaves a heavy sigh. "I feel so fucking stupid."

Smirking, I say, "Calm the fuck down, Tripod."

"Waverly."

"I was trying to get your attention. It will all be okay. We'll deal with it if it comes up. No more freaking out. If you are so worried, there is a morning-after pill."

"No morning-after pill. We will be okay. I know this is only our first date, but I love you."

"I know you do. I'm not ready to say that yet. I think it is too soon. But you can say it as often as you want. I like hearing it."

"No pressure, Peaches."

"I know." I lean against him. "Now, not to change the subject, but does this mean that we can go without a condom? That dick is too fucking good to cover up."

Chuckling, he says, "Whatever you want, love. I'm not going anywhere."

EPILOGUE

Our one year anniversary is coming up fast. I am thankful my stalker—I mean, Valentine Crush turned out to be the love of my life. Coben's momma raised him right. When he said, I will get used to being treated like a queen; he wasn't lying.

He makes dinner almost every night. Refusing to let me cook after coming home from work. I've tried to beat him home to surprise him with a meal and have succeeded maybe three times. I get nighty back rubs, which always leads to fantastic sex.

Today is Friday. I'm ready to have this weekend off. I want to spend days wrapped in Coben's arms. I leave at two and can't wait.

"Waverly!"

"Ren!" Laughing, I yell back at him.

"When are you out of here?"

"About an hour," I say after checking the time.

"Okay. Enjoy your weekend. I have a client about to come in, and I won't see you before you leave."

"Sounds good," I reply. "I'll see you Monday."

"Day off for me. There is a letter on the front counter for you. It came in the mail."

I walk to the lobby, and there lays a thick red envelope with my name written on it. I smile when I realize it is from Coben. It brings back a sense of déjà vu when I slip in the letter opener.

Waverly

Waverly,

I have had you for one year. My love for you has only grown. There is only one thing that we need to fix, and that is your last name. It may be cliché that I am asking on Valentine's Day but fuck it. Waverly, will you do me the honors of becoming Mrs. Tripod?

Love,
You're Valentine Crush

P.S. Look up and quit laughing.

I can't stop laughing. Only Coben would write fuck it in a marriage proposal and use his nickname. I glance up. Down on one knee, Coben holds a ring and a bag of gummy worms, smiling.

"Well?"

Pausing for effect, I toy with my lip. When he's suffered enough, I gush, "Yes!"

He jumps up, wraps his arms around me, and we spin in a circle. We're both laughing and crying. I hear clapping behind us. I turn, and there are Ren and Laken with big smiles, clapping.

"You knew?" I accuse.

"Yep," they say in unison.

"Wait. Are you Ren's client?" I ask Laken.

She nods shyly.

"Don't fuck up, Ren," I say, giving him a severe look. Then I point at Laken. "Don't break his heart."

"I won't," he says sincerely.

"I won't." she agrees.

"So," I grin, "we have a wedding to plan ASAP."

"Damn, babe. Can't wait to be Mrs. Tripod?" he jokes.

Pausing, I place a hand on my belly. "I don't want to have a big gut when I walk down the aisle."

"What?" Laken screeches in excitement.

"Are we pregnant?" Coben asks with love in his eyes.

"About six weeks. I wanted to tell you in a cute way. But now that we are engaged, I figured you needed to know sooner rather than later."

He bends down and kisses my flat belly. "We need to get you two home," he says in a questioning voice when he said two.

"We won't know for sure until our first ultrasound in four weeks," I assure him. "One will be plenty."

"I can't wait."

"Me either. Take me home so we can start our happily ever after," I say, kissing him.

"Yes, ma'am."

ACKNOWLEDGMENTS

I want to thank my husband and my children for always cheering me on. Without you three, I wouldn't be doing half the things I do. My nose would be stuck in a book. I also want to thank my very best friends for always pushing me to keep writing and helping me with ideas. Veronica, Rebecca, Elizabeth, and Joyce, I love you ladies so much.

Thank you to my Beta Reader Tiffany Robinson and all of my ARC readers. I would like to also thank my author friends that have been supporting me every step of the way! I love you and your books. Lastly, I want to thank all of my readers that will read anything I write. Your support means so much to me.

ALL ABOUT ROSE BUSH

Rose resides in Ohio with her husband and her two children. Rose is an avid reader. Some of her favorite authors are Jessica Wayne, Helen Hardt, Rebecca Morman, Katy Rose, and Lynn Hammond. When she isn't reading, she makes graphics, bottle cap keychains, and bookmarks for fun. She has an unhealthy love of Reese's cups and sweet tea.

- facebook.com/RoseBushBAPA
- goodreads.com/rosebush2020
- bookbub.com/authors/rose-bush

BOOKS BY ROSE BUSH

Basic Bitch Apocalypse

The definition of a basic bitch is a woman who is condescending, predictable, and is unoriginal in style, interests, or behaviors. That's what it says in the slang dictionary. To me, that is a very good definition, but they left out the leggings, fuzzy boots, messy buns, and the pumpkin spice lattes.

Have you ever wondered what would happen to the basic bitches when they ran out of the pumpkin spice lattes? Well, I know what happens, and this is the story of what will happen.

Broken Dreams- Book 1 of Charlie's Girls

Since birth, Lauren suffered. Despised by neglectful and abusive parents. Abducted and renamed by Charlie...her savior. Her story is not a happy one.

Through grit and will, Lauren does unspeakable things to gain her freedom.

The past haunts, creeping in shadows, lurking behind closed eyelids. Lauren remains trapped in a cycle of broken nightmares. Her secret past eats and gnaws at her insides, but whom can she tell? Her best friend, Violet? Certainly not her dream man, Layne. Something must change, or Lauren will never shed her shame...her wreckage.

Shattered Reality- Book 2 of Charlie's Girls

Charlotte was a straight-A student that had big dreams and ambitions. Then she bumped into a nightmare, and her life took a horrific turn. Will she find an escape? Will she be sold? Will she find love in the most unexpected place?

Fractured Destiny- Book 3 of Charlie's Girls

I went with you willingly.

You asked me to stay.

I thought you loved me, but you threw me away.

Think again bitch... I'll make you pay.

Made in the USA
Columbia, SC
19 January 2025